D1541610

MaDCaP CaPeRs

Poison Ivy's Big Boss in Bloom

by Michael Anthony Steele
illustrated by Sara Foresti

Batman created by Bob Kane with Bill Finger

STONE ARCH BOOKS
a capstone imprint

Published by Stone Arch Books, an imprint of Capstone.
1710 Roe Crest Drive
North Mankato, Minnesota 56003
capstonepub.com

Library of Congress Cataloging-in-Publication Data
Names: Steele, Michael Anthony, author. | Foresti, Sara, illustrator.
  | Kane, Bob, creator. | Finger, Bill, 1914-1974, creator.
Title: Poison Ivy's big boss in bloom / by Michael Anthony Steele ;
  illustrated by Sara Foresti.
Description: North Mankato, Minnesota : Stone Arch Books, an
  imprint of Capstone, [2022] | Series: Harley Quinn's madcap capers
  | "Batman created by Bob Kane with Bill Finger." | Audience: Ages
  8–11. | Audience: Grades 4–6. | Summary: Harley Quinn and
  Poison Ivy escape from Arkham Asylum and head back to Ivy's
  hideout; however, Harley proves to be a demanding roommate, so
  Ivy helps her take over a carnival and even grows her plant versions
  of Batman and Robin to boss around—but when Poison Ivy feels she
  has done enough and withdraws from the field, Harley discovers
  that being a criminal boss is a lot more difficult than she imagined.
Identifiers: LCCN 2021030700 (print) | LCCN 2021030701 (ebook) |
  ISBN 9781663975300 (hardcover) | ISBN 9781666329698 (paperback)
  | ISBN 9781666329704 (pdf)
Subjects: LCSH: Harley Quinn (Fictitious character)—Juvenile fiction.
  | Poison Ivy (Fictitious character)—Juvenile fiction. | Batman
  (Fictitious character)—Juvenile fiction. | Supervillains—Juvenile
  fiction. | Superheroes—Juvenile fiction. | CYAC: Supervillains—
  Fiction. | Superheroes—Fiction. | LCGFT: Superhero fiction.
Classification: LCC PZ7.S8147 Po 2022 (print) | LCC PZ7.S8147
  (ebook) | DDC 813.6 [Fic]—dc23
LC record available at https://lccn.loc.gov/2021030700
LC ebook record available at https://lccn.loc.gov/2021030701

Designed by Kay Fraser

TABLE OF CONTENTS

Harley Quinn's Madcap Capers

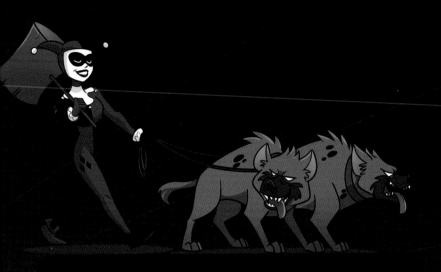

Dr. Harleen Quinzel was once a successful psychiatrist at Gotham City's Arkham Asylum. But everything changed when she met the Joker. As the Clown Prince of Crime shared his heartbreaking—yet fake—story of a troubled childhood, Harleen's heart melted. She soon helped the Joker escape and joined him as a jolly jester with a calling for crime. Now she clowns around Gotham City, and these are . . .

HARLEY QUINN'S MADCAP CAPERS!

CHAPTER 1

Dinner Out

Harley Quinn held her own throat with both hands. "Ack!" she croaked. "Can't breathe . . ." Her eyelids fluttered as she coughed and sputtered.

The Arkham Asylum orderly outside Harley's cell simply rolled her eyes and shook her head. "I'm not falling for it, Harley."

Harley staggered off her bunk and pawed at the air in front of her. "Who's that? Is someone there?"

Harley opened the door to see another orderly already there. The man sat with his back to her as he watched a television screen.

"That was fast," the man said without looking back. "You passed out those meals in record time."

Harley cleared her throat. "Uh, yeah," she said, trying to sound like Maggie. "But Mister J's . . . I mean . . . the Joker's cell is empty."

Still glued to the television, the man gave a dismissive wave. "He broke out last week."

Harley's mouth fell open in surprise. He was gone? Without her? She closed her mouth and her jaw tightened. How could Mister J leave her behind like that?! She trembled with rage. She had to get out of there, find him, and give him a piece of her mind. But how could she escape?

That's when Harley spotted a small potted plant next to the television screen. Its leaves were wilted and its one flower had lost most of its petals.

"Your plant doesn't look so good," Harley said.

The orderly reached over and spun the small clay pot. "Yeah, I brought it to cheer up the place," he said. "But it doesn't get enough light in here."

Harley marched over and snatched up the pot. "I know someone who can help with that."

She was already out the door when the orderly turned around. "Wait, what?"

Harley sprinted back down the corridor. She slid to a stop in front of one of the cells and whipped out the keycard.

CLANK! The door sprang open to reveal a thin man in a gray jumpsuit inside the cell. "Riddle me this," the man said. "What has four legs, wheels, and flies?"

"Oh, boy," Harley said. "Wrong cell."

She slammed the door shut and moved to the next one.

CLANK! This time, a woman with red hair and green skin was inside. She also wore a gray jumpsuit as she sat on her bunk. Poison Ivy glanced up with a puzzled expression.

"Harley?" she asked.

"Hi-ya, Red!" Harley greeted her as she bounded into the cell. "Look! I brought you something!"

Ivy took the pot and examined the wilted plant. "Oh, you poor thing. What have they done to you?"

Ivy touched one of the drooping leaves and the entire plant perked right up. The leaves stiffened and bright new petals sprouted from the flower.

Suddenly, multiple footsteps echoed in the corridor. Soon, three orderlies skidded to a halt in front of Ivy's cell. They each held nightsticks and glared in at Harley and Ivy.

"Get back to your cell now, Quinn," one of the orderlies commanded. "Don't make us force you."

Harley turned back to Ivy and grinned.

A thin smile pulled at Poison Ivy's lips. "Thanks for the gift, Harls."

Harley stepped aside as Ivy stood and placed the potted plant on the floor. Then she tapped the plant's flower with her finger.

POP!

Poison Ivy glanced up and saw another vine slowly wrapping around Harley's body. "Oops," she said. "Sorry about my security system." Ivy snapped her fingers and the vines plopped Harley onto a comfy chair.

"No, I mean what am I going to do about finding Mister J?" Harley asked.

Ivy went back to watering her plants. "Why do you want to find him so badly?" she asked.

Harley shrugged. "Cuz he's the boss."

"Why don't you become your own boss?" Ivy asked.

"Gee," Harley replied as she scratched her head. "I never thought of that."

"After all, he left you locked up in Arkham after he escaped," Ivy said as she moved to another plant.

Harley frowned. "Yeah. What do I need him for?!"

"Exactly," Ivy agreed. "You're the Cupid of Crime. The Mistress of Mayhem."

Harley sprang from the chair. "You're right, Red. I don't need him at all. I can be my own boss!" Harley skipped over to Ivy. "But I tell you what I do need . . . I need to get my babies out of lockup."

Ivy raised an eyebrow. "Your hyenas?"

"Yup!" Harley nodded. "And I know just the person to help me spring them." She leaned her head onto Ivy's shoulder. "After all, I helped that same certain someone break out of Arkham quite recently."

Ivy's shoulders slumped. "All right."

* * *

That night, Harley Quinn and Poison Ivy headed over to the Gotham City Zoo. Outside the gate, Ivy had a large tree lower a thick branch to the ground. Ivy and Harley hopped on, and the tree carried them over the gate before gently placing them on the other side.

"This way, Red," Harley said as she led the way. "Sneak, sneak, sneak!" She giggled as she tiptoed down the walkway.

"You have to be quiet," Ivy whispered.

"Oh, yeah," Harley said. "Sneak, sneak, sneak," she whispered as she continued to tiptoe.

Before long, they reached a cage with two dark figures huddled inside. Harley ran up to it and the creatures charged the bars. Their mouths stretched wide, showing rows of sharp teeth.

Harley knelt down and jutted her arms into the cage. "Crackers! Giggles! Did you miss Mama?" The hyenas cackled with laughter as she ruffled their furry coats.

"Make it fast, Harls," Ivy said, glancing around. "I have a bad feeling about this."

Harley gave the animals a final scratch before moving to the cage's gate. She pulled out a lock pick and went to work on the lock.

SHHHH-PANG! A sharp object flew by her head and struck the side of the cage. It was a metal weapon in the shape of a bat—a Batarang!

Harley spun around. "What's the big idea?!"

Batman and Robin stood atop a nearby elephant enclosure. Their capes fluttered as they gazed down at the two criminals.

"I thought this would be your first stop, Harley," Batman said.

Robin put his hands on his hips and chuckled. "It didn't take the World's Greatest Detective to figure that one out."

The crime fighters swooped to the ground.

"You're both going back to Arkham," Batman declared. "Now!"

Harley rolled her eyes and shook her head. "Buy me some time, would you, Red?" She went back to the lock.

Ivy raised both hands above her head. "Gladly."

Before the Dynamic Duo could make a move, the trees on either side of them came to life. They swiped at the heroes with thick branches. Batman ducked under one while Robin somersaulted over another.

Ivy laughed as she made the trees uproot themselves and lumber toward the crime fighters. Batman and Robin were dwarfed beneath the woody giants.

Meanwhile, Harley had picked the lock and freed her hyenas. They followed her as she dashed to nearby cages and freed other animals. She released two elephants, a rhinoceros, and a hippopotamus. The herd of animals charged toward the Dynamic Duo.

Harley dusted her hands together. "That should keep them busy for a while," she said. She reached down and patted the heads of her two hyenas. "Come on, Red. Let's make like a tree and leave." Harley giggled along with the hyenas as they darted toward the exit. "Get it? Because trees have leaves."

"I get it, Harley," Ivy said as she ran after her. "Believe me, I get it!"

CHAPTER 3

Location, Location, Location

"Aw, come on, Red," Harley said. "With all these plants around here, surely you can spare one stick so the boys can play fetch."

"Absolutely not," Ivy said as she gently clipped the leaves from a tall bush. "And with the arrival of your . . . babies . . . don't you think things are a little . . . crowded around here lately?"

"No way," Harley said as she sat on the floor, scratching Giggles behind the ears. "They don't take up that much room. And they're both housebroken and everything."

Ivy frowned as Crackers walked out from behind a particularly wilted potted tree. "I think you and I have two very different ideas of what *housebroken* means," Ivy murmured.

Crackers launched himself at a nearby plant and began tugging at one of its vines.

Ivy groaned as she put down her shears. "All I'm saying is that, if you want to be your own crime boss, shouldn't you have a place of your own?" She strolled over to the hyena and snatched the vine from his mouth.

Harley sprang to her feet. "My own hideout!" she shouted. "What a great idea! My own secret lair!"

Ivy smiled. "It makes sense."

Harley bounded over to Ivy and gave her a hug. "And I just know, with your help, we'll be able to find the perfect spot!"

"With my help?" Ivy asked, raising an eyebrow.

"Sure," Harley replied. "After all, it was my help that got you out of Arkham Asylum. And that's what friends do . . . help each other!"

Ivy's shoulders slumped. "Fine."

* * *

Ivy and Harley spent the rest of the day searching for the perfect hideout. They visited an abandoned balloon factory, an old rubber duck plant, and an old trampoline park.

Harley enjoyed bouncing on one of the few trampolines that didn't have holes in it. Crackers and Giggles leaped into the foam pit and began chewing up the pieces of foam.

"Well?" Ivy asked with her arms crossed. "What do you think?"

BOING! BOING! BOING! BOING!

"It's okay . . . ," Harley replied between bounces. "I was just hoping . . . for something . . . a little more . . . exciting."

"Aw, come on, Harls," Ivy said. "This has you written all over it."

"I want . . . to keep . . . looking," Harley said before somersaulting off the trampoline. She flew through the air and landed next to Ivy. Harley whistled and her hyenas scrambled out of the foam pit and joined her.

Ivy sighed. "All right."

They searched all over Gotham City for the rest of the day. Harley found something wrong with every place they came across. She didn't get excited until they came upon a carnival in full swing. Harley ran up to the gate, gazing at all the flashing lights, listening to all the loud music, and smelling all the carnival food.

"It's perfect!" Harley said.

Ivy scratched her head. "Didn't you and the Joker use a carnival as a hideout before?"

"Yeah," Harley replied. "But that was an abandoned carnival. This one is so much better." She ran through the gate. "All the roller coaster rides and cotton candy I want!"

Ivy and the hyenas ran after Harley. They caught up to her as she approached three large men standing beside a ticket booth.

"Hey, who's in charge here?" Harley asked them.

"I am," replied the man in the middle.

Harley tapped the man's nose with one finger. "Wrong answer. I am!"

The men looked at each other in surprise before bursting into laughter. When they finally stopped, the man in the middle nodded at the other two. "You guys want to escort these two and their pets off my lot?"

As the two men stepped forward, Ivy held up one hand and blew on her open palm. Bright-yellow pollen flew from her hand and dusted the men's faces. They coughed and sputtered before their expressions went blank.

"Now," Ivy said, "who's in charge?"

The three men pointed at Harley. "She is," they said in unison.

"Yay!" Harley clapped as she bubbled with excitement.

Ivy followed Harley and the hyenas around the grounds as she pointed out all the changes she wanted to make. Thanks to Ivy's special pollen, all the carnival workers let them go wherever they wanted.

"I want a big picture of me on top of the fun house and on the center of the Ferris wheel," Harley announced. "And I want all the bumper cars painted black and red!"

Harley didn't seem to notice how all the guests ran away screaming as they strolled through the carnival. She also didn't see the frightened expressions of the four people on the roller coaster as two Super-Villains and two hyenas climbed into the last two cars. The mesmerized worker pulled the lever, beginning the ride.

KLACK-KLACK-KLACK-KLACK-KLACK!

"As hideouts go, don't you think this place is a little . . . high profile?" Ivy asked as the roller coaster climbed the track.

Harley took a big bite of cotton candy. "Why's that?" she asked with her mouth full.

Poison Ivy pointed to the rise above them. "That's why."

Batman and Robin swung into view. Their capes fluttered as they landed atop the track.

"Enough of this, Harley," Batman ordered. "You two are going back to Arkham now!"

Harley stood and angrily threw away her cotton candy. "Aw, you have to ruin everything, don't ya?!"

Robin crossed his arms. "When it comes to criminals like you . . . it's what we do best!"

Harley sighed. "I guess you were right, Red," she told Ivy. "Let's get out of here."

Poison Ivy raised a hand and a giant beanstalk erupted from the ground below.

WHOOSH!

It grew thicker and taller until it was even with the climbing roller coaster. Four vines unfurled and snaked toward them. They plucked Harley, Ivy, and the hyenas out of the cars and gingerly carried them away from the crime fighters.

"This should keep you busy," Ivy said as a fifth vine shot out from the beanstalk. Batman and Robin dove off the track as it whipped toward them. They clung to the side of the vine as it slammed down onto a lower part of the roller coaster track.

SMASH!

A large gap appeared in the track. The roller coaster topped the hill and then rolled down the track, building up speed. The passengers screamed as they hurtled toward the twisted and mangled rails below.

POP! POP!

Batman and Robin fired their grapnels at the nearby Ferris wheel. Once their lines were secure, they swung up and each snatched two of the frightened riders from the cars. When they were clear of the cars, the roller coaster hit the gap in the rails. It flew off the track, spun in midair, and smashed into an empty ticket booth.

KRASH!

By the time the crime fighters had the guests safely on the ground, Poison Ivy and Harley Quinn were long gone.

CHAPTER 4

Help Wanted

"That was the last one," Harley said, bouncing on the newly repaired trampoline. "It works like a charm!"

Poison Ivy had spent all morning helping set up the abandoned trampoline park as Harley's new hideout. With the help of Ivy's vines, they had cleaned up the place and repaired all the equipment.

"I'm glad you like it," Ivy said. "Now, I think we're finally even for . . ."

"You know what this place is missing?" Harley interrupted. She leaped off the trampoline and landed next to Ivy. "What kind of big crime boss would I be without any people to, you know, boss around?"

Ivy raised her eyebrow. "You mean thugs and goons?" She glanced around at the empty space and chuckled. "What are you going to do? Hold auditions or something?"

Harley's eyes lit up. "What a wonderful idea!"

Ivy held both hands out. "Wait a minute, I was just . . ."

Harley grabbed one of Ivy's hands and pulled her toward the door. "Come on! Let's get the word out!"

* * *

For the rest of the day, Harley dragged Ivy all over Gotham City. They visited all the seedy hangouts looking for any and all out-of-work Super-Villain crews. By the time night fell, Harley's hideout was full of men and women whose bosses were either locked up in Arkham or who were simply looking to join a new crew.

There were several men and women dressed in green and covered in question marks. They were from the Riddler's crew. The goons who used to work for Two-Face wore suits that were nice on one half and tattered on the other. Some former Bane bodybuilders still sported their wrestling masks, while a few of the Penguin's former flunkies wore tuxedos and carried rolled-up umbrellas. There were even a couple of thugs in clown masks who used to work for the Joker.

"We definitely have to work on the uniform situation," Harley whispered to Ivy as they sat atop a trampoline.

Harley scrambled to her feet. "All right, everyone. If you're going to be on the Harley Quinn crew, you have to be tough." She folded her arms and scanned the crowd. "So . . . let's see what ya' got!"

Everyone glanced around, confused. After a moment, a Bane bodybuilder shrugged and then picked up a guy wearing a clown mask. She spun him over her head before flinging him into the Two-Face crowd.

BAM! They went down like bowling pins.

That's all they needed to get going. A brawl erupted between all the colorful thugs and goons.

SMAK! BAM! BOOM! BAM! BAM!

The Bane bodybuilders put their best wrestling moves on half of the Two-Face minions. The hoodlums in clown masks slugged it out with the other half. The former Riddler goons used their question mark canes to fence with the Penguin mob and their umbrellas. It was a regular flunky fight fest!

Harley sat back down beside Poison Ivy. "I don't know, Red. They're okay, I guess." She shook her head. "But how are they going to be against Batman and Robin?"

Ivy smiled. "I think I can help with that." With a flick of her wrist, several vines erupted from the floor. They twisted and tangled until they began to take the shape of two people. The vines wove a long, flowing cape before ending in sharp thorns atop the taller figure's head. The shorter figure had a smaller woven cape flowing behind him.

Harley grinned when she realized that Ivy had created plant versions of the Dynamic Duo themselves.

Harley giggled and sprang to her feet. She put fingers in the corners of her mouth and whistled loudly. The battling brutes halted and looked up at her.

"Okay, that's good enough for round one," Harley said. "But for your final test . . ." She pointed at Ivy's newest creations. "You have to beat . . . Plant-Man and Buddin!"

The crowd looked at the two green figures with confusion. Then the plant-based Super Heroes struck fighting poses. The mass of minions yelled as they charged toward them.

"I can't believe it," Harley said as she watched the new brawl. "Those two fight as well as the real Batman and Robin!"

Buddin quickly somersaulted over the Bane brutes before taking out the Two-Face goons. Meanwhile, Plant-Man raised an arm and shot a vine toward the ceiling the same way Batman used his grapnel. The vine latched onto the rafters and hoisted up the figure. Then Plant-Man swung into the middle of the Riddler and Penguin thugs. It dodged umbrellas and question mark canes while delivering several well-placed punches.

BAM! POW! BAM!

In no time, the plant-based Super Heroes were the last ones standing. Most of the goons ran out of Harley's hideout. Those who didn't were knocked out cold.

Harley squealed and ran up to Plant-Man and Buddin. She grinned as she put her arms around Ivy's newest creations. "I think I just found my crew!"

CHAPTER 5

The Big Bloom

"All right, Harls," Poison Ivy said as she headed toward the door. "If you keep them watered, your new crew should last you a very long time."

Harley bounded over to Ivy. "You can't leave yet, Red," she said, holding up her phone. "I just found the perfect score!" The screen showed a photo of a multicolored flower. "The Gotham City Botanical Gardens are showing off a rare clown orchid."

"Look, Harley, I have my own plans . . ."
Ivy began.

"But it's the perfect heist for a team-up,
don't ya think?" Harley interrupted. She
lowered her phone and gazed at Ivy with big,
sad eyes. "Come on, Red. Just one big score
together. Pretty please . . ." Harley hung her
head and kicked at the floor. "After all, if it
wasn't for me, you'd still be all locked up at
Arkham."

Ivy threw her head back and growled with
frustration. "Fine!" She glared at Harley and
held up a finger. "But this is the last thing.
After that, we're even, right?"

"You bet," Harley said, giving Ivy a big
hug. "Even Steven!"

* * *

The next day, several botanical garden guests gathered around the newest display. The stone pedestal held a large plant with a single colorful flower. The orchid had five bright yellow petals, each with purple stripes running down the middle. The flower's multicolored center resembled a face, so the entire orchid looked like a little clown.

"It's remarkable," a woman commented.

"It's stunning," a man added.

"It's mine!" Harley declared as she strolled into view.

There were cries of alarm as Harley, Ivy, and the hyenas pushed through the crowd. Harley was about to reach out and take the plant when two security guards rushed in.

"Hold it right there," one of the guards ordered.

Harley gave Ivy a nudge. "Get a load of this guy." She glanced over her shoulder and gave a whistle.

Two figures swooped in from the trees.

"Look!" shouted one of the guests. "It's Batman and Robin!"

Harley chuckled. "Guess again."

The plant versions of the crime fighters squared off against the security guards. The two men glanced at each other before charging. Plant-Man flipped one guard over its shoulder, while Buddin swept the legs out from under the other. After a very brief struggle—*BAP! BAM! KA-POW!*—the guards were out cold.

Harley snatched the orchid from the pedestal and held it up. "I have the perfect place for this little baby in my new hideout."

"Look!" repeated one of the guests. "It's Batman and Robin!"

Harley rolled her eyes. "Okay, look . . . I told you already . . ."

"Uh, Harls," Ivy interrupted.

She pointed to the two figures running toward them from the parking lot. It was the real Batman and Robin. The Batmobile had barely rolled to a stop behind them.

"All right, fellas," Harley said to her new crew. "You were made for this. Go get 'em!"

Plant-Man and Buddin darted toward the approaching crime fighters.

"Am I seeing things?" Robin asked as he charged toward a plant version of himself.

Batman's lips tightened. "It looks as if Poison Ivy came up with a new trick."

With a flick of his wrist, the Dark Knight sent three Batarangs flying toward his green look-alike.

WHP-WHP-WHP!

The weapons hit their marks, but had no effect. Plant-Man leaped into the air, spread its cape wide, and came down on Batman. The two tumbled across the ground.

Meanwhile, Robin was tangling with the plant-based Boy Wonder. They each blocked punches and dodged kicks.

BAF! WHP! WHOP!

The two fighters were evenly matched and neither one seemed to gain the upper hand.

"I know I'm not supposed to beat myself up," Robin said. "But this is ridiculous." He blocked another punch. "Plus, I'm not getting anywhere."

"Me neither," Batman agreed as he repelled a kick from the green version of himself. "Want to trade?"

"Good idea," Robin said. He grabbed the shoulders of the smaller plant figure and flipped it toward Batman.

The Dark Knight performed a flying kick, striking Plant-Man's chest. The green version of himself tumbled toward Robin.

The Boy Wonder launched a pair of bolas toward Plant-Man's feet. The balls at the end of the rope wrapped around the creature's legs, and it slammed to the ground.

With its legs trapped, the plant version of Batman raised an arm at Robin. It shot out a vine the way the real Batman would fire his grapnel.

WHOOSH!

The Boy Wonder leaped into the air,
dodging the attack. Plant-Man fired again
and again, but Robin narrowly avoided each
snaking vine.

Meanwhile, Batman blocked a flying
kick from Buddin. The smaller creature
somersaulted backward, landing on the
ground. It ran in for another attack.

"Coming to you," Batman announced. He
caught the plant version of Robin by the leg
and flung it toward the real Robin.

The Boy Wonder launched himself into
the air as Plant-Man shot out another vine.
Robin leapfrogged over Buddin, and the vine
wrapped around his plant look-alike. The
vine retracted, tangling the two plant figures
together.

WHIP!

Batman flung another Batarang at them. This one was special. It had a flashing red light and beeped loudly.

BEEP-BEEP-BEEP-BEEP-BEEP . . . BOOM!

The Batarang exploded, taking the two fake crime fighters with it. Batman and Robin shielded themselves with their capes as they were pelted by a barrage of branches, thorns, and twigs.

* * *

With the Caped Crusaders occupied, Harley, Ivy, and the hyenas ran out of the botanical garden. They crossed the street and darted down the busy Gotham City sidewalk. People screamed and scattered as they got out of the way.

"That was a close one," Harley said as she held the orchid tightly. "I think I'm going to need a new crew though."

"This was the last favor, remember?" Ivy said. "I have plans of my own, Harley."

VROOOOM!

Just then, the Batmobile raced past. It made a U-turn ahead of them and screeched to a stop.

SCREEEEEE!

Crackers and Giggles raced toward the vehicle. Their lips curled back to expose mouths full of sharp teeth as they cackled crazily.

A small slot on the front of the Batmobile slid open.

POW!

A black ball shot out of the slot. As it neared the attacking hyenas, it expanded into a large net. The net wrapped around the beasts, stopping them in their tracks.

The Batmobile's main hatch slid open and the Dynamic Duo sprang out. Their capes flowed behind as they landed on the sidewalk.

Harley grabbed Ivy's arm. "How about one more favor, huh?"

Ivy frowned. "Harley . . ."

"After all," Harley continued, "if it wasn't for my help at Arkham . . ."

"Harley!" Ivy interrupted.

"Oh, please," Harley begged. "Pretty please? With sugar on top?"

"Okay," Ivy agreed. "But this is really it."

The Queen of Green closed her eyes and the orchid began to grow in Harley's hands. Its pot burst as its roots shot down to the sidewalk to form two legs. As the plant grew, Harley barely had time to scramble onto its back before it towered over the scene.

"You're on your own now, Harls," Poison Ivy said as she made her escape.

"Thanks, Red!" Harley shouted as she rode the giant plant. It lumbered toward Batman and Robin, striking down at them with its newly formed fist.

FOOM! The crime fighters barely leaped clear as the fist smashed the sidewalk.

"Whoo-hoo!" Harley cheered.

Robin looked down at the pair of bolas in his hands. "I don't think these will work on this one."

"Think bigger," Batman said. "I'll get it into position."

POP! Batman fired his grapnel at a nearby building. Once it was attached, he shot off the ground as the tool retracted. The Dark Knight barely dodged a swipe from the giant orchid.

"Who's the big boss now?!" Harley asked as the orchid turned to attack the swinging Super Hero.

"Now, Robin," Batman ordered as he landed on the sidewalk behind the beast.

The Boy Wonder leaped into the Batmobile and hit a switch.

FOOM! A giant pair of bolas launched from the front of the vehicle. The huge balls wrapped thick cords around the monster's legs. It lost its balance and toppled forward.

"Uh-oh," Harley said as she rode the giant plant down.

The orchid slammed to the ground, and Harley tumbled across the sidewalk. Before she could get to her feet, Batman was there.

"It's time to go back, Harley," he said as he slapped handcuffs on her.

"I guess you're right, Bats," Harley replied. "This boss business is hard work, ya know? I could really use a rest." She smiled up at him. "Maybe I'll make it back to Arkham for dinner. I wonder what it'll be . . . steak or lobster?"

POISON IVY

REAL NAME: Pamela Isley
OCCUPATION: Professional Criminal, Botanist
BASE: Gotham City

BIOGRAPHY: Unaffected by plant toxins and poisons since birth, Pamela Isley's love of plants began to grow like a weed at an early age. She eventually became a botanist, or plant scientist. Through reckless experiments with various plant life, Pamela Isley's skin itself has become poisonous. Her venomous lips and poisonous plant weapons present a real problem for Batman. But Ivy's most dangerous quality is her extreme love of nature—she cares more about the smallest seedling than any human life.

HARLEY'S FRIENDS AND FOES

FRIENDS

Harley & Poison Ivy

Harley & The Joker

Catwoman

Giggles, Harley, & Crackers

FOES

Batman

Robin

Batgirl

Batwoman

Batwing

BIOGRAPHIES

photo by M. A. Steele

MICHAEL ANTHONY STEELE has been in the entertainment industry for more than 27 years, writing for television, movies, and video games. He has authored more than 120 books for exciting characters and brands including Batman, Superman, Wonder Woman, Spider-Man, Shrek, Scooby-Doo, LEGO City, Garfield, Winx Club, Night at the Museum, and The Penguins of Madagascar. Steele lives on a ranch in Texas, but he enjoys meeting his readers when he visits schools and libraries all across the country. For more information, visit MichaelAnthonySteele.com.

photo by Sara Foresti

SARA FORESTI was born in northern Italy. She attended a graphic design school close to home and became a freelance graphic designer upon graduating. While Sara really liked the field of design, she soon discovered the amazing world of children's illustration and fell in love with it. Sara now lives in Canada and works as a children's illustrator. Her other projects include greeting cards, educational and fiction books, digital apps and videos, and comics.

GLOSSARY

audition (aw-DISH-uhn)—a tryout performance for an actor or musician

bola (BOW-la)—a throwing weapon made of weighted balls connected by cords

botanical (buh-TAHN-i-kuhl)—having to do with plants

grapnel (GRAP-nuhl)—a grappling hook connected to a rope that can be fired like a gun

hacienda (ha-see-EN-da)—the Spanish name for the main house on an estate

hyena (hi-EE-na)—a wild animal that looks somewhat like a dog

orderly (OR-dur-lee)—a hospital attendant who cleans and does other jobs

pendant (PEN-duhnt)—a hanging ornament worn on a necklace

pollen (POL-uhn)—tiny grains that flowers produce

projectile (pruh-JEK-tuhl)—an object, such as a bullet or missile, that is thrown or shot through the air

tuxedo (tuhk-SEE-doh)—a man's jacket, usually black with satin lapels, worn with a bow tie for formal occasions

TALK ABOUT IT

1. Why does Poison Ivy agree to help Harley? Should she have refused to help her? What might have happened if she had?

2. Harley visits a few different locations while looking for her perfect hideout. Which one do you think would have been the best headquarters for her? Explain your answer.

3. Why do you think Batman and Robin are so evenly matched when fighting Plant-Man and Buddin? Where do you think the vegetable villains got their skills?

1. Imagine what would happen if Plant-Man and Buddin went on their own adventures. Would they be heroes or villains? Write a short story featuring this plant-based pair!

2. Super-Villain henchmen often wear clothing that resembles their boss in some way. If Harley gathered her own crew of henchmen, what would they wear? Write a paragraph describing their clothing and draw a picture of them.

3. At the end of the story, Harley is being taken back to Arkham Asylum. But what if she escapes on the way there? Write a new chapter describing how Harley escapes and what she does next.

READ THEM ALL!

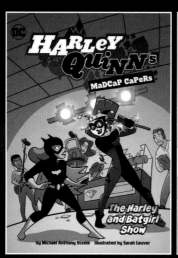

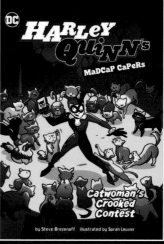

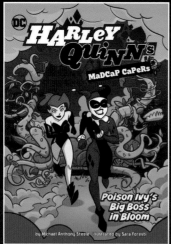